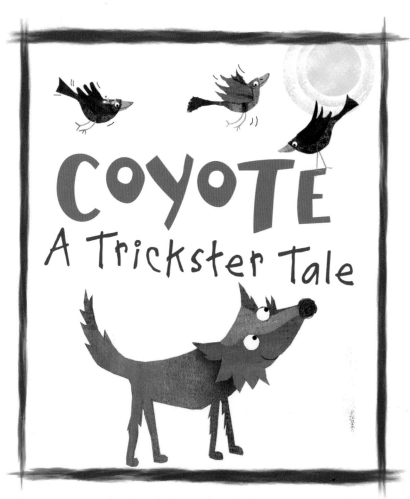

COYOTE
A Trickster Tale

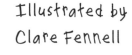

Written by
Sam Besson

Illustrated by
Clare Fennell

Lee Aucoin, *Creative Director*
Jamey Acosta, *Senior Editor*
Heidi Fiedler, *Editor*
Produced and designed by
Denise Ryan & Associates
Illustration © Clare Fennell
Rachelle Cracchiolo, *Publisher*

Teacher Created Materials
5301 Oceanus Drive
Huntington Beach, CA 92649-1030
http://www.tcmpub.com
Paperback: ISBN: 978-1-4333-5608-7
Library Binding: ISBN: 978-1-4807-1730-5
© 2014 Teacher Created Materials

Contents

The ancient Pueblo people lived in the American Southwest, where the days are hot and the nights are cold. The Pueblo are known for many things, and telling stories is one of them. This is a retelling of a story about Coyote.

Chapter One

A Nose for Trouble

One day, as Coyote was passing by a spiky Joshua tree, he saw a flock of crows singing and dancing, chanting, and laughing. He turned and crept up close to watch them.

Coyote had a nose for trouble, and he was following his nose again! He forgot that the crows were always trying to trick him. He watched as the crows flew into the sky and headed toward the canyon.

If only I could fly, he thought. *That would mean I would be the greatest coyote ever born. Maybe the crows could show me how.*

So Coyote called to the crows as they circled the canyon, "I'd love to join you!"

Old Man Crow laughed to himself and said to his flock, "Let's have some fun with this silly creature."

7

Chapter Two

Wings

Old Man Crow plucked a shiny
black feather from one of his wings.
He told his flock to do the same.

9

They each flew down and stuck their feathers into Coyote. It hurt a lot! He tried not to cry, but his eyes watered and his nose twitched. The crows laughed among themselves. "What a silly coyote he is!" they said to each other.

"Now, you are ready to fly," Old Man Crow told Coyote.

"Oh, thank you!" said Coyote, "Soon, I will soar into the sky and be the greatest coyote ever born!"

Then, the crows began to dance. They hopped on one foot, and then the other. Coyote tried to dance, too. He was completely out of step, although he thought he was a brilliant dancer. He smiled proudly to himself.

"I think I *am* the greatest coyote ever born," he told Old Man Crow, as he danced dangerously close to the edge of the steep canyon.

Suddenly, the crows flew into the sky like a shiny black cloud rising from the ground. Coyote tried to follow, but it was impossible! He was completely off balance. He couldn't lift himself off the ground even an inch.

"Wait! Don't leave me!" he cried, as he stumbled around. He tripped over his feet and fell. It hurt, and Coyote felt very sorry for himself.

Chapter Three

The Greatest

The birds flew back and gazed at Coyote lying on the ground. They chuckled at the state he was in. Coyote looked back at them sadly.

Old Man Crow said, "No wonder you couldn't fly. You need more feathers so you have two wings! You only had enough for one wing."

Hopeful once more, Coyote asked the birds to help him again. So the birds plucked more feathers from their wings and stuck them into Coyote's skin. Coyote tried not to yelp with pain as the crows smiled to themselves.

"Oh, thank you so much," said Coyote. "Now, I will surely be able to fly! I will soar like an eagle and glide like a hawk. I *will* be the greatest coyote ever born!"

It didn't take long for the crows to become bored and a little annoyed by Coyote's boastfulness. Teasing him wasn't as fun as they thought it would be. They began to dance and chant again, trying to ignore him.

But Coyote joined in immediately, flapping his feathers and making an awful yapping noise. He thought he had a beautiful singing voice, but the crows thought it was dreadful.

Chapter Four

Coyote Colors

Irritated, the crows stopped
dancing and chanting. They rose
into the air and flew out over
the canyon.

Coyote tried to fly with them. He ran, dipped his feathers up and down, hopped from one foot to the other, and then he flew—just for a few short moments. He didn't soar like an eagle. He didn't glide like a hawk. Coyote flapped feebly in the air for a few feet before falling over the edge of the canyon.

"*Ahhhhhhhh!*" he yowled as he plummeted toward the ground. "Help me!" he howled, but the crows did not swoop down to carry him. They circled around him and took back their feathers as fast as they could. Coyote fell even more rapidly.

In fact, Coyote fell so quickly that the motion caused his tail to catch on fire! Luckily, he fell into a pool of water, and only the tip of his tail was burnt. As he dragged himself out, he could hear the crows laughing. He watched them fly away. Coyote tried to run after them, but he tripped and fell in the dusty dirt.

Slowly, he picked himself up and loped home sadly. Coyote, who wanted to fly like the crows, soar like the eagles, and glide like the hawks, was completely covered in dust. The tip of his tail was burnt. He was a complete mess.

To this day, Coyote is the color of dust. To this day, his bushy tail has a burnt black tip. And to this day, Coyote still follows his nose. He has a nose for trouble, and he *always* finds it.

Sam Besson lives in a seaside town in Victoria, Australia. When he was young, he tried to learn something about every country in the world, even those that had names he couldn't pronounce. He didn't manage to find out about every single one, but he has since traveled to more than twenty countries, where he loves to record people's stories.

Clare Fennell lives in Leicestershire, England. Clare works mainly in collage, recycling bits of magazines, fabric, newspaper, and anything else she can find! She mixes the collages with painted elements, and then finishes her work digitally. Clare illustrated *Cuckoo, Cuckoo: A Folktale from Mexico* for Read! Explore! Imagine! Fiction Readers.